W9-BAW-947
DISCARDED FROM THE
PORTVILLE FREE LIBRARY

THE GUMDROP TREE

THE GUM

ILLUSTRATED BY JULIA GORTON

ELIZABETH SPURR
DROP
TREE
Hyperion Books for Children
New York

Printed in Hong Kong. For
information address Hyperion
Books for Children, 114 Fifth
Avenue, New York, New York
10011.

FIRST EDITION

1 3 5 7 9 10 8 6 4 2

Library of Congress Cataloging-in-
Publication Data

Spurr, Elizabeth.
The gumdrop tree/Elizabeth Spurr;
illustrated by Julia Gorton — 1st ed.
p. cm.
Summary: When her father gives
her a bag of colorful, sugary
gumdrops to eat, a little girl decides
to plant them instead.
ISBN 0-7868-0008-9 (trade) —
ISBN 0-7868-2004-7 (lib. bdg.)
[1. Candy — Fiction.
2. Gardening — Fiction.]
I. Gorton, Julia, ill. II. Title.
PZ7.S7695Gu 1994
[E] — dc20 93-38234
CIP AC

The
artwork
for
each
picture
is
prepared
using
airbrushed
acrylic
on
paper.

This book is set in Futura Medium.

Design and typography
by Julia Gorton

For Jim
— E.S.

To my little gumdrops, Ivy and Raleigh
— J.G.

My father
brought me a
bag of gumdrops.
RED,
YELLOW,
ORANGE,
PURPLE,
GREEN,
AND BLACK.

They sparkled
with sugar. They
looked so
sweet and
good.

They looked so sweet and good I could not eat them. Because then they would be all gone.

I put them in a row.

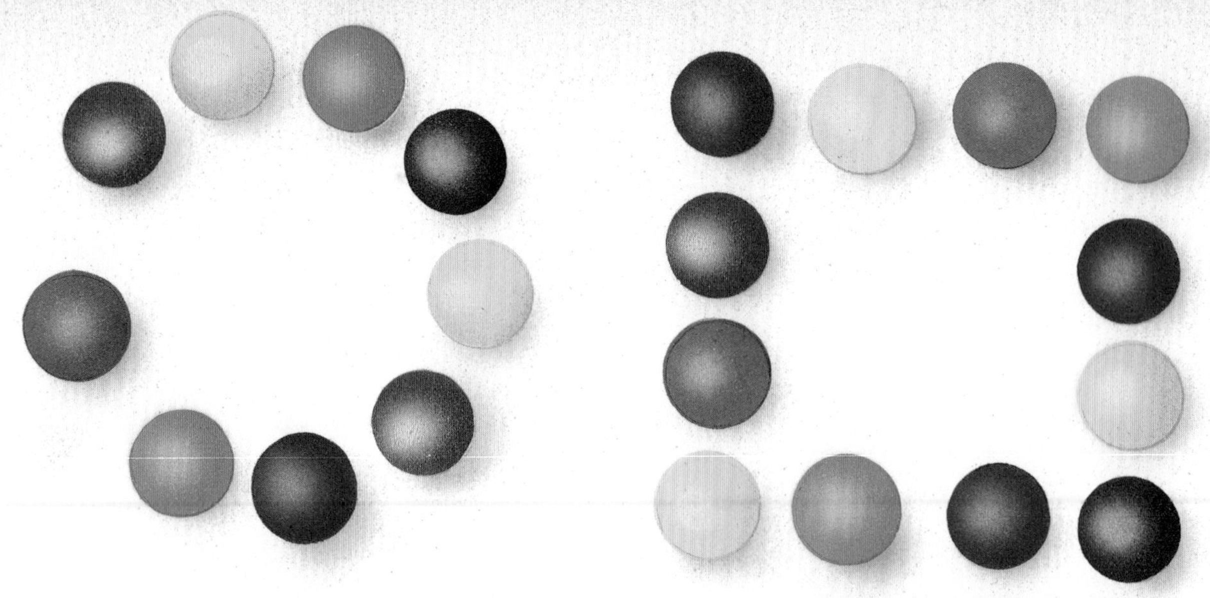

I laid them in a circle.

I made a square

and two triangles.

I piled them up.

I knocked them down.
Still I did not eat them.
They would taste so
sweet and good.
But then they
would be
all gone.

I had an idea.

I would plant them in the garden. I would plant them near the peach tree I had grown from a seed. I grew it by watering and watching and waiting. The peaches tasted sweet and good. But now they were all gone.

I dug a hole.
I dropped the gumdrops in.
Every day I watered.
And watched.

I covered them with dirt.

Now they were all gone. But not for long.

And waited.

Until finally...

"Mom! Dad!
Come see!
I planted all
my gumdrops.
Soon I'll have a
gumdrop tree."

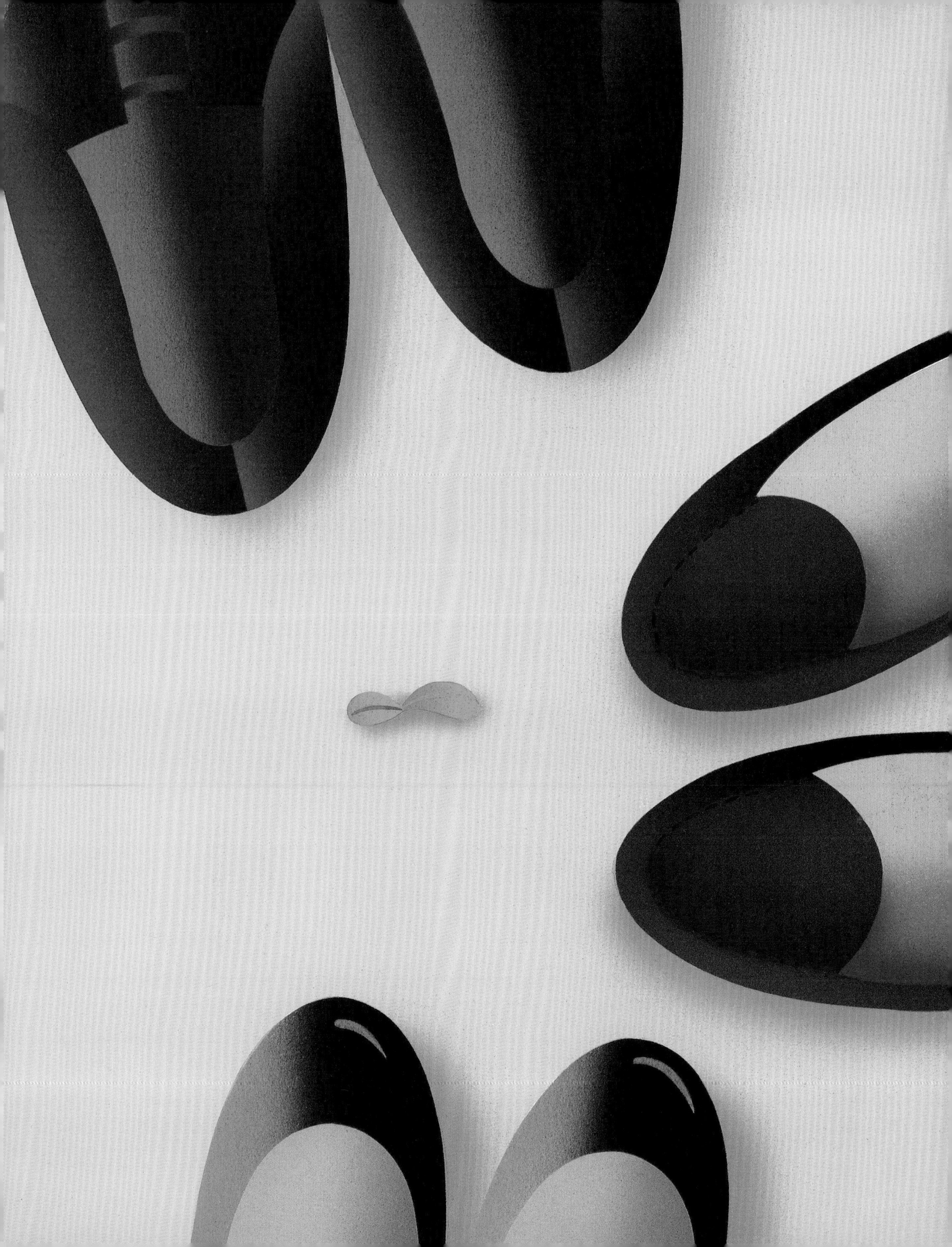

My mother and father
looked at the sprout.
They smiled at each other.
"A gumdrop tree.
What a good idea."

I watered.
And watched.
And waited.

A shoot.

A blade.

A stalk.

I watered.
Watched.
Waited.

A stalk
with branches.
Branches
with buds.

Buds
with leaves.

But no
gumdrops.

Not even one.

I did not water anymore.

I did not watch.

I did not wait.

Dumb gumdrop tree.

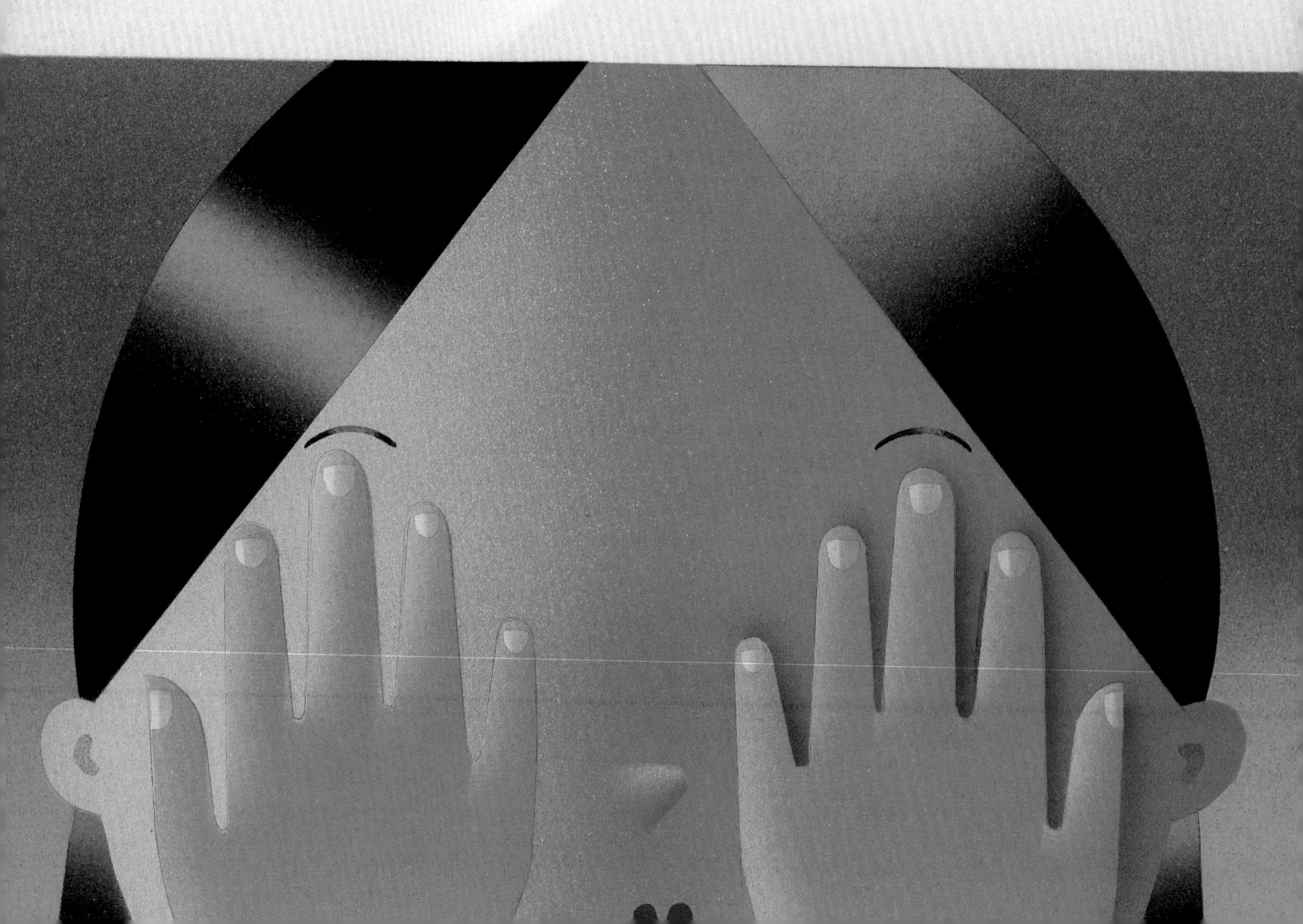

The rains came. The sun shone.

The tree grew taller.

I did not watch. I did not wait.

But once in a while

I took a peek.

Nothing but branches, buds, blossoms. Until one day...

"Mom! Dad!
Come see.
Come see my
gumdrop tree!"

Gumdrops! Red, yellow, orange, purple,

green, and black. They sparkled with sugar.

"Why don't you pick them?" asked my father.

My mother said, "They look so sweet and good."

I picked the gumdrops. Red, yellow, orange, purple, green, and black.

I put them in a row. I laid them in a circle. I made a square and two triangles. I piled them up. I knocked them down.

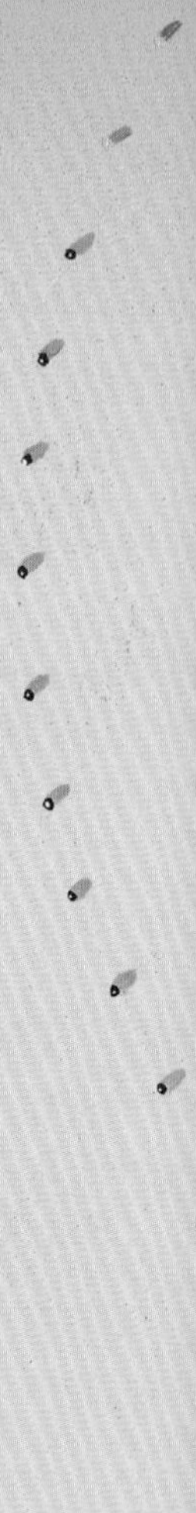

Then...

I ATE
THEM

Red, yellow,
orange, purple,
green, and black.
They tasted sweet
and good.
And soon
they were all gone.